Laugh-Out-Loud
Road Trip
Jokes for Kids

LAUGH -Out- LOUD ROAD TRIP JOKES for KIDS

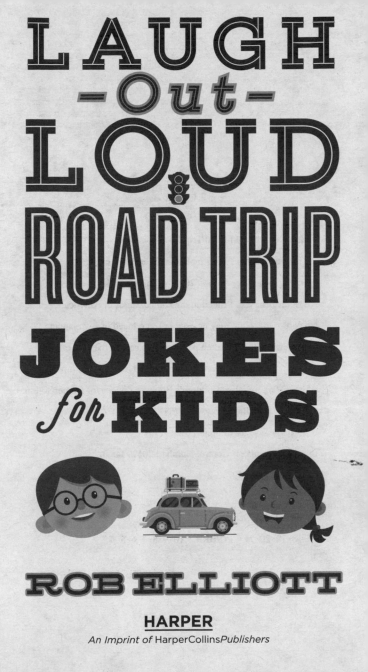

ROB ELLIOTT

HARPER

An Imprint of HarperCollinsPublishers

Library of Congress Control Number: 2017934826

ISBN 978-0-06-249793-2

Typography by Gearbox

17 18 19 20 21   PC/BRR   10 9 8 7 6 5 4

❖

First Edition

Joanna, Josh, Cassie, Emma, Leah, Anna, and Mason: I wouldn't want to travel through any adventure in life without you!

- -

Q: Where do couples travel to get married?

A: To Marry-land! (Maryland)

Q: Where is the best place to go shopping for clothes?

A: New Jersey.

Q: Which mountain has never been climbed?

A: Mount Never-est.

Q: Where's the best place to get a kidney transplant?

A: Oregon. (organ)

- -

Q: Where do people like to vacation over and over?

A: Michigan . . . and igan and igan.

Q: What do you call a country with pink automobiles?

A: A car-nation.

Q: What is the cleanest state?

A: Wash-ington.

Knock, knock.

Who's there?

S'more.

S'more who?

Do you want to hear s'more road trip jokes?

Q: **How did the zookeeper calm down the wild elephant?**

A: With a trunk-quilizer.

Q: **Why did Cinderella buy a camera?**

A: So she could find her prints charming.

Knock, knock.

Who's there?

Zeke.

Zeke who?

Zeke and you will find!

Knock, knock.

Who's there?

Needle.

Needle who?

I needle little help getting this door open.

CAN YOU TAKE THE TRAIN
to the
LINCOLN MEMORIAL?

Tic - **TAC** - *Toe*

- -

Q: Why did the man cry when he ran out of cola?

A: Because it was soda-pressing.

Knock, knock.

Who's there?

Launch.

Launch who?

Can we stop for launch yet?

Q: Why did the clock go on vacation?

A: It needed to unwind.

Knock, knock.

Who's there?

Anita.

Anita who?

Anita pull over and use the bathroom!

Q: **What does a *Tyrannosaurus rex* eat while it's camping?**

A: Dino-s'mores!

Knock, knock.

Who's there?

Spell.

Spell who?

W-h-o.

Q: **What do you eat when you visit the Florida Everglades?**

A: Marsh-mallows.

Q: **What do sheep always take on a camping trip?**

A: Their baa-ckpacks.

Q: Why can't you take a skunk on vacation?

A: Your trip will stink!

Q: Why should you always listen to porcupines?

A: They have a lot of good points.

Knock, knock.

Who's there?

Dewey.

Dewey who?

Dewey get to play at the beach this summer?

Knock, knock.

Who's there?

Alpaca.

Alpaca who?

Alpaca suitcase for our vacation.

- -

Knock, knock.

Who's there?

Whale.

Whale who?

Whale all you want. I'm not opening the door!

Knock, knock.

Who's there?

Iowa.

Iowa who?

Iowa lot of money, so I can't afford a vacation this year.

Knock, knock.

Who's there?

Jamaica.

Jamaica who?

Please don't Jamaica me tell more knock-knock jokes!

14

Knock, knock.

Who's there?

Alaska.

Alaska who?

Alaska you to tell me a joke next time!

Q: Why don't sand dollars take a bath?

A: Because they wash up on the shore.

Nick: Do you know the capital of Alaska?

Sam: Yes—don't Juneau?

Sara: What is the capital of Oregon?

Sophia: O.

Knock, knock.

Who's there?

Mushroom.

Mushroom who?

How mushroom do you have left in your suitcase?

Will: Where are there oranges, beaches, and Mickey Mouse?

Bill: In Flori-duh!

Q: What did America say to England when it called after midnight?

A: "Europe?"

Q: What is a sailor's favorite snack?

A: Ships and salsa.

Q: What goes up and down but never moves?

A: A flight of stairs.

Q: How do crabs buy their toys?

A: With sand dollars.

Q: Where does a triceratops like to go swimming?

A: At the dino-shore.

Q: What did the poodle say to the Dalmatian?

A: "I have a bone to pick with you!"

- -

Q: Why wouldn't the jellyfish go down the water slide?

A: Because he was spineless.

Q: Why did the choir go on a cruise?

A: They wanted to hit the high Cs. (seas)

Knock, knock.

Who's there?

Taco.

Taco who?

I could taco 'bout my family vacation all day.

Knock, knock.

Who's there?

Window.

Window who?

Window we finally get there?

Q: What does a trash collector eat for lunch?

A: Junk food.

Knock, knock.

Who's there?

Lettuce.

Lettuce who?

Lettuce go to the beach!

Q: Where is the slipperiest place in the world?

A: Greece.

Mason: Can we have a fish for dinner?

Lucas: Sure, I'll set an extra place at the table.

Knock, knock.

Who's there?

Wheel.

Wheel who?

Wheel be going on our trip soon!

Knock, knock.

Who's there?

Quiche.

Quiche who?

Quiche me before you leave!

Q: Why did the mummy keep hugging her kids good-bye?

A: She thought they were eerie-sistible.

Q: What did the goldfish say after its trip?

A: "What a fin-tastic vacation!"

Q: What kind of money is easy to burn?

A: In-cents.

Knock, knock.

Who's there?

Joe King.

Joe King who?

I'm not Joe King—let me in!

Q: What do spiders eat at a picnic?

A: Corn on the cobweb.

- -

Q: When do birds fly south?

A: In flock-tober.

Q: What happened when the beagle played in the snow?

A: It turned into a chili dog!

Q: How did the famer get rich?

A: He sold his corn stalks. (stocks)

Mason: I ran over a skunk with my bike!

Josh: That stinks.

Q: Why wouldn't the cow get a job?

A: Because he was a meat loafer.

HANG-MAN

- -

DOTS!

Each player takes a turn connecting one dot to another dot. The game is played until all the dots become boxes. The player with the most boxes completed at the end is the winner.

Knock, knock.

Who's there?

Gopher.

Gopher who?

I'd gopher a trip abroad if I were you.

Knock, knock.

Who's there?

Pudding.

Pudding who?

I'm pudding away my books for the summer!

Q: Why does coffee get in trouble?

A: Because it's not tea. (naughty)

- -

Knock, knock.

Who's there?

Stopwatch.

Stopwatch who?

Stopwatch you're doing and open the door!

Q: What do you call a crocodile that's always picking fights?

A: An insti-gator.

Q: When is your money stuck in the bank?

A: When you can't budget. (budge it)

Q: What does an archer wear to the ball?

A: A bow tie.

- -

Q: Why did the cow yell at the chicken?

A: It was in a bad moo-d.

Q: Why couldn't the pirate play cards?

A: He was standing on the deck.

Q: Where does a sailor go when he's sick?

A: To the dock.

Q: What is an artist's favorite kind of juice?

A: Crayon-berry.

Knock, knock.

Who's there?

Sweet tea.

Sweet tea who?

Could you be a sweet tea and open the door?

- -

Q: **What do you call a reindeer that swims in the ocean?**

A: Ru-dolphin.

Q: **How does an astronaut pay for his coffee?**

A: With Star-bucks!

Q: **What did the watch say to its grandfather clock?**

A: "I want to wind up like you!"

Q: **Why did the pilot paint his jet?**

A: He thought it was too plane.

Q: **How do artists get to work?**

A: They go over the drawbridge.

- -

Q: Why do cows believe everything you say?

A: Because they're so gulli-bull.

Knock, knock.

Who's there?

Tibet.

Tibet who?

Early Tibet, early to rise.

Patient: I broke my leg in two places! What should I do?

Doctor: Don't go to those places!

Q: What do chickens like to eat for dessert?

A: Bak, bak, baklava.

- -

Q: Why did the whale buy a violin?

A: So it could join the orca-stra.

Q: What do you get when you cross a dentist and a boat?

A: A tooth ferry!

Jen: Do you want to see the volcanoes in Hawaii?

Jill: I'd lava to!

Q: Why did the wheels fall off the car?

A: They were tired!

Q: Why did the meteorite go to Hollywood?

A: It wanted to be a star.

- -

Q: Why did the horse keep falling down?

A: It wasn't very stable!

Q: What kind of train needs a tissue?

A: An achoo-choo train!

Q: What do you call a hamburger in space?

A: A meat-eor!

Q: Why don't turtles use the drive-through?

A: They don't like fast food.

**Mom: Why do we have to stop at every filling
station on the highway?**

Dad: It isn't polite to pass gas.

Q: **What do you get when it rains in Paris?**

A: French puddles. (poodles)

Q: **How do you hide in the desert?**

A: Wear camel-flage.

Q: **How do you motivate a lazy mountain?**

A: Light a fire under its butte!

Q: **What kind of car does Mickey Mouse drive?**

A: A Minnie-van.

Q: **Where do elephants keep their spare tires?**

A: In their trunks.

Q: What do you call a horse in space?

A: A saddle-lite.

Q: What do cars wear to stay warm?

A: Hoodies.

Q: How do marine biologists feel about the ocean?

A: They're fin-atics!

Q: How did the lettuce win the race?

A: It got a head start!

Q: How do smart students travel to school?

A: On scholar-ships!

- -

Cowboy Hank: Round up the cattle! Round up the cattle! Round up the cattle!

Cowboy Frank: I herd you the first time.

Q: What do taxi drivers eat for dinner?

A: Corned beef and cab-bage.

Q: Why didn't the melons get married?

A: Because they cantaloupe.

Q: Why don't stars carry luggage on vacation?

A: Because they're traveling light.

Emma: How many antelope live in Africa?

Leah: Probably a gazelle-ion!

Q: **How do you get an astronaut's baby to sleep?**

A: You rocket.

Q: **What kind of boat do you hit with a stick on your birthday?**

A: A pin-yacht-a.

Q: **What do you call a happy cowboy?**

A: A Jolly Rancher.

Knock, knock.

Who's there?

Wafer.

Wafer who?

I've been a wafer too long—let me in!

𝒯𝒾𝒸 - **TAC** - 𝒯𝑜𝑒

CAN YOU FLY
to
YELLOWSTONE NATIONAL PARK?

Q: How does Saturn clean its rings?

A: With a meteor shower!

Q: When do scuba divers sleep underwater?

A: When they're snore-keling.

Q: Why did the mechanic stop pumping gas?

A: It was a tank-less job.

Q: What kind of car does a dog like to drive?

A: A Land Rover.

Q: Why was the astronaut hungry?

A: Because he missed his launch.

Q: What's a tornado's favorite game?

A: Twister!

- -

Q: Why did the lettuce turn around?

A: It was headed in the wrong direction.

Q: What do you call a crazy spaceman?

A: An astro-nut.

**Q: What does the queen of England wear
on vacation?**

A: A tea shirt.

Q: Which cowboy looks like all the others?

A: The Clone Ranger.

Q: What's an astronaut's favorite drink?

A: Gravi-tea.

Q: Where does a bee wait for a ride?

A: At the buzz stop.

Q: Where does a dog leave its car?

A: In the barking lot.

Q: What did George Washington call his false teeth?

A: Presi-dentures.

- -

Q: What happened when the clam went to the gym?

A: He pulled a mussel.

Q: What is something you always leave behind at the beach?

A: Your footprints.

Q: What is a pirate's favorite Christmas carol?

A: "Deck the Halls."

Q: Why did the hamburger go to the gym?

A: He wanted better buns.

Q: How are flowers like the letter *A*?

A: Bees come after them.

Q: Why do dogs have a great attitude?

A: They like to stay paws-itive.

Q: Why did the criminal go to the gym?

A: He wanted abs of steal.

Q: What kind of bugs like sushi?

A: Wasa-bees.

Q: What did the ocean do when the kids left the beach?

A: It waved good-bye.

- -

Annie: What should I wear when I visit Disneyland?

Amy: A Minnie-skirt!

Q: Why do sharks swim in salt water?

A: Pepper water makes them sneeze!

Q: Why do wasps need to go on vacation?

A: Because they're always busy bees.

Q: Why couldn't the astronaut remember anything?

A: He didn't have enough brain space.

Q: Why couldn't the cat go on the field trip?

A: It forgot its purr-mission slip.

- -

Q: Why did the surfer go to the hair salon?

A: She wanted a permanent wave.

**Q: What do you get when you cross a
strawberry with a propeller?**

A: A jelly-copter!

Q: What kind of fruit do you find in a volcano?

A: A lava-cado!

**Q: What do you get when you cross a king
with a boat?**

A: Leadership!

Q: Where does a farmer stay on vacation?

A: At a hoe-tel.

**Q: Why did the tugboat and the yacht
get married?**

A: They were in a loving relation-ship.

Q: What does it take to work for the railroad?

A: Lots of training.

Q: How do you send a knight on a mission?

A: You give him a re-quest.

Missy: What do you think of the Grand Canyon?

Mandy: It's gorge-ous!

- -

Q: Why did the astronaut leave the party?

A: He needed some space.

Q: Why can't fishermen get along?

A: They're always de-baiting.

Q: What do you get if you give diamonds to an ambassador?

A: Peace and carats. (peas and carrots)

Q: **How do you know if someone ran into your car?**

A: Look at the evi-dents.

Q: Why do fishermen always tell the truth?

A: They keep it reel.

- -

Q: Why are trains so focused?

A: They need to stay on track.

Q: Why is the post office a friendly place?

A: It has a lot of outgoing mail.

Knock, knock.

Who's there?

Avenue.

Avenue who?

Avenue packed for your trip yet?

Q: Why were the kids wet when they got to school?

A: They'd ridden in a car pool.

- -

Q: Where do astronauts listen to music?

A: On Neptune.

Q: What do you call a storm that is always rushing around?

A: A hurry-cane.

Q: How do astronauts throw a party?

A: They planet.

Q: Why wouldn't the acrobat perform in winter?

A: He only knew how to do summer-saults.

- -

Q: Why was the sailor upset over his report card?

A: His grades were at C level.

Q: What do you get when you cross a crocodile and a GPS?

A: A navi-gator.

Q: What does Santa wear to the beach?

A: His swim-soot.

Q: Where do penguins go to vote?

A: The South Poll.

Q: How do you get to your accountant's office?

A: In an income taxi.

- -

Q: Where do pirates go to the bathroom?

A: On the poop deck.

Q: What happens when your noodles catch a cold?

A: You get macaroni and sneeze!

Q: Why did the beaver cross the road?

A: To get to the otter side.

Q: What happens when a toad is nervous?

A: It gets worry warts!

Q: How do fish get around the busy ocean?

A: They hail a crab.

Knock, knock.

Who's there?

Izzy.

Izzy who?

Izzy doorbell working or should I

keep knocking?

Q: Why did the lumberjack fall asleep?

A: He was board!

HANG-MAN

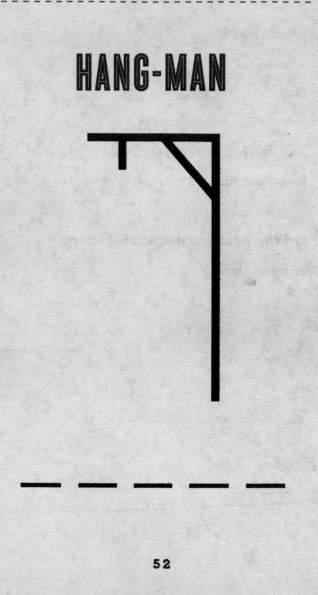

DOTS!

Each player takes a turn connecting one dot to another dot. The game is played until all the dots become boxes. The player with the most boxes completed at the end is the winner.

Q: How does a chicken build a house?

A: It lays bricks.

Knock, knock.

Who's there?

Russell.

Russell who?

Russell up some grub. I'm hungry!

Knock, knock.

Who's there?

Handsome.

Handsome who?

Handsome keys over and I'll let myself in.

- -

Q: How was the horse able to pay for all its hay?

A: It had a stable income!

Q: Where did the butcher take his wife on

a date?

A: To the meatball.

Knock, knock.

Who's there?

Fixture.

Fixture who?

Fixture doorbell and I won't have to knock

so much!

- -

Q: What did Darth Vader say to his son?

A: "I wish you'd be a trooper!"

Q: Why was the tightrope walker stressed out?

A: He was having trouble balancing his schedule.

Knock, knock.

Who's there?

Honeydew.

Honeydew who?

Honeydew you know who's knocking at the door?

Q: Why did the kids get in trouble at Disney World?

A: They were trying to be Goofy!

- -

Joe: Jim, does your doctor do house calls?

Jim: Yes, but your house has to be pretty sick before he'll come over.

Q: What superhero do you want on your baseball team?

A: Batman.

Q: Why couldn't the baker get to his bagels?

A: Because they had lox on them!

Q: Where do birds go for a break?

A: On a re-tweet. (retreat)

- -

Q: What does a pig say on a hot summer day?

A: "I'm bacon out here!"

Knock, knock.

Who's there?

Belle.

Belle who?

Belle is fixed, so you don't have to knock!

Q: What do you get when you cross a cow with a roll of tape?

A: A beef stick.

Q: How does the sun kiss the moon?

A: It puckers its ec-lips.

- -

Q: What do you call tiny glasses?

A: Speck-tacles.

Q: What kind of bird do you eat for dessert?

A: A mag-pie.

Q: Why does everyone ask for Mickey
  Mouse's autograph?

A: Because he's fa-mouse.

Q: What do you call a zombie elephant?

A: Gro-tusk.

- -

Q: Why did the race-car driver pour stew on his motor?

A: He wanted to soup up the engine.

Q: Why do skunks always show off?

A: They want to be the scent-er of attention.

Q: What did the paper say to the pen?

A: "Write on!"

Q: When is a boxer a comedian?

A: When he delivers a punch line!

Knock, knock.

Who's there?

Leaf.

Leah who?

Leaf the key under the mat so I don't have to knock!

Q: What kind of car does a tiger drive?

A: A Cat-illac.

Q: Why did Frosty move in with his friends?

A: So he wouldn't feel so ice-olated.

- -

Q: Why was the Tin Man sad on Valentine's Day?

A: Because he was heartless.

Q: What do you call a pig in the dirt?

A: A groundhog.

Q: Why did the snail stay home from school?

A: He was feeling a bit sluggish!

Tongue Twisters

Flat atlas

Pack black pants

Sharks floss fast

Scared squirrels scram

Cranky cramped campers

- -

Knock, knock.

Who's there?

House.

House who?

House it going?

Travis: I was going to tell you a rumor about germs.

Scott: Why don't you?

Travis: I'm afraid it might spread.

Q: What was Noah's job in the Bible?

A: Ark-itect.

Q: What kind of bird do you send on a quest?

A: A knight owl.

Q: What do you get when you throw cabbage in the snow?

A: Cold slaw.

Q: Why did the orange juice have to go to principal's office?

A: It wouldn't concentrate in class!

Q: Why did the cow cross the road?

A: To get to the udder side.

- -

Q: Why don't canaries want to pay for a vacation?

A: Because they're cheep!

Max: What would happen if a snake swam across the Atlantic?

Jax: It would make hiss-tory!

Q: What do you get when a witch loses her magic?

A: A hex-a-gone.

Q: Where do horses live?

A: In neighborhoods.

- -

Q: Why did the banker go to the football game?

A: He wanted his quarterback!

Q: What is a beluga's favorite drink?

A: Mana-tea.

Q: Where can you find a beaver and

an astronaut?

A: In otter space!

Knock, knock.

Who's there?

Gladys.

Gladys who?

I'm Gladys time for summer vacation!

- -

Knock, knock.

Who's there?

Pasture.

Pasture who?

Is it pasture bedtime?

Q: Why is it hard to be a firefighter?

A: You get fired every day!

Q: What's a frog's favorite kind of music?

A: Hip-hop!

CAN YOU TAKE THE SUBWAY *to the* **STATUE OF LIBERTY?**

Tic - **TAC** - Toe

Knock, knock.

Who's there?

Sarah.

Sarah who?

Is Sarah doctor in the house?

Knock, knock.

Who's there?

Russian.

Russian who?

I'm Russian to pack so I don't miss my flight!

Knock, knock.

Who's there?

Anita.

Anita who?

Anita come in so I can talk to you!

Knock, knock.

Who's there?

Iran.

Iran who?

Iran all the way here.

Knock, knock.

Who's there?

Abbott.

Abbott who?

It's Abbott time you answered the door!

Knock, knock.

Who's there?

Yukon.

Yukon who?

Yukon open the door anytime now!

Knock, knock.

Who's there?

Cher.

Cher who?

Cher would be nice if you could join us on vacation!

- -

Knock, knock.

Who's there?

Heaven.

Heaven who?

You heaven a hard time opening the door?

Knock, knock.

Who's there?

Theodore.

Theodore who?

Theodore is jammed and I can't get it open!

Knock, knock.

Who's there?

Hugo.

Hugo who?

When Hugo on vacation I'll miss you!

Q: Why did the chicken quit laying eggs?

A: It was eggs-hausting!

Q: What do they eat in the navy?

A: Submarine sandwiches.

Knock, knock.

Who's there?

Cain.

Cain who?

Cain you tell me some more knock-knock jokes?

George: Have you ever seen a catfish?

Henry: Yes, but I don't think it caught anything.

Q: What kind of lion can you have in the house?

A: A dandelion!

Q: How do you find a train that's lost?

A: Follow its tracks.

Q: Where do you take a fish for an operation?

A: To the sturgeon.

Q: What do you eat for lunch in the desert?

A: Sand-wiches.

- -

Q: Where do Sharpies go on vacation?

A: Pen-sylvania.

Q: What does a cow do on January first?

A: It makes its moo-year's resolution.

Q: What goes tick, tick, woof, woof?

A: A watchdog.

Q: What do you get when you combine a snail and a porcupine?

A: A slowpoke!

Josh: Let me tell you about my underwear.

Jeff: Okay, but please keep it brief. . . .

Q: What do you call a bull that's scared all the time?

A: A cow-ard!

Q: What happens if a kangaroo can't jump?

A: It feels un-hoppy.

Q: When can't you trust a painter?

A: When he's a con artist.

Q: How do you reward the best dentist in town?

A: Give her a plaque!

- -

Q: Why didn't the man trust his bushes?

A: They seemed shady.

Q: When is a car like a frog?

A: When it's being toad!

Q: What do you call a wise dentist?

A: A philo-flosser.

Q: Where do plants like to go to school?

A: The Ivy League.

Q: When is it hard to tell the truth?

A: In Fib-ruary.

Q: What kind of candy do boxers eat?

A: Jawbreakers!

Q: What did the snowman say when he got
   new glasses?

A: "I-cy!"

Knock, knock.

Who's there?

Saul.

Saul who?

I Saul you were home, so I knocked on the door.

HANG-MAN

- -

DOTS!

Each player takes a turn connecting one dot to another dot. The game is played until all the dots become boxes. The player with the most boxes completed at the end is the winner.

Knock, knock.

Who's there?

Ketchup.

Ketchup who?

Let's ketchup with each other soon.

Knock, knock.

Who's there?

Doris.

Doris who?

The Doris locked or I wouldn't be knocking!

Q: What kind of monkey do you see up in the sky?

A: A hot-air baboon.

- -

Q: What do dogs have for their birthdays?

A: Pup-cakes!

Knock, knock.

Who's there?

Johana.

Johana who?

Johana open the door so I can come in?

Q: Why did the clock get sent to the

    principal's office?

A: It wouldn't stop tocking in class!

Q: Why was the banjo sad?

A: Everyone was picking on it.

Q: **How does a slug cross the ocean?**

A: In a snailboat!

Knock, knock.

Who's there?

Utah.

Utah who?

Utah me how to drive—thanks!

Q: **What happened when the duck went to the doctor?**

A: It got a clean bill of health.

Q: **Why is it hard to beat barbers in a race?**

A: They take shortcuts!

- -

Knock, knock.

Who's there?

Lena.

Lena who?

Lena little closer and I'll tell you a secret.

Q: Why was the corn feeling sad?

A: It was the laughing-stalk of the farm.

Knock, knock.

Who's there?

Rwanda.

Rwanda who?

Rwanda let me in?

- -

Q: What happens when rabbits fall in love?

A: They live hoppily ever after.

**Q: What do you get when you cross a frog and
a chair?**

A: A toadstool.

Dan: Can you help me find a new dentist?

Sam: You should try mine—he knows the drill!

Knock, knock.

Who's there?

Luke.

Luke who?

Luke outside and you'll see!

Q: How much did the wasp pay for its honey?

A: Nothing, it was a free-bee.

Q: Where does a rabbit go when he needs glasses?

A: A hop-thalmologist.

Q: Where does a peach take a nap?

A: On an apri-cot.

Q: What do boxers eat for dinner?

A: Black-eyed peas.

Q: What kind of dog is always sad?

A: A melan-collie.

Q: What kind of people never get upset?

A: No-mads.

Q: Why did the cow need a tissue?

A: For its moo-cus.

Q: What do you get when you cross a carrot and a pair of scissors?

A: A parsnip.

- -

Q: What kind of bread is the cheapest?

A: Pumper-nickel.

Q: What kind of cheese stays by itself?

A: Prov-alone.

Q: What do you call a cow with a telescope?

A: A star grazer.

Q: What does a crocodile drink at the gym?

A: Gator-ade.

Q: What do clowns eat for lunch?

A: Peanut butter and jolly sandwiches.

Knock, knock.

Who's there?

Elsa.

Elsa who?

Me! Who Elsa do you think it would be?

Q: What do a dog and a watch have in common?

A: They both have ticks.

Q: What did the hen say to its chick?

A: "You're a good egg."

Knock, knock.

Who's there?

Amish.

Amish who?

Amish you and wish you were here!

Q: Why couldn't the spider get anywhere?

A: It was just spinning its wheels.

Q: What do lamps wear to the beach?

A: Shades.

Q: What do TVs wear to the beach?

A: Sun-screen.

Q: What's a bunny's favorite toy?

A: A hula hop.

Q: What's a farmer's favorite movie?

A: *Beauty and the Beets*.

Q: What do you call songs you compose in bed?

A: Sheet music.

Q: Why did the shark cross the road?

A: To get to the other tide.

Knock, knock.

Who's there?

Pencil.

Pencil who?

Your pencil fall down if you don't wear a belt.

- -

Knock, knock.

Who's there?

Wayne.

Wayne who?

Wayne will ruin our day at the beach!

Q: Why did the deer go to the orthodontist?

A: Because it had buck teeth.

Q: What do dogs and sheep have in common?

A: They both have fleece. (fleas)

Q: Who do you call if it's raining cheeseburgers?

A: A meat-eorologist.

CAN YOU DRIVE
to the
GRAND CANYON?

Tic - **TAC** - *Toe* -

Q: Why was the clock bored?

A: It had too much time on its hands.

Q: Why did the butcher follow the detective?

A: He wanted to go on a steak-out.

Q: What did the dog have to do before going out to play?

A: Ask his paw first.

Q: Why did the pineapple cake turn upside down?

A: It saw the cinnamon roll!

Q: Why couldn't the oyster talk?

A: It clammed up!

Knock, knock.

Who's there?

Butch, Jimmy, and Joe.

Butch, Jimmy, and Joe who?

Butch your arms around me, Jimmy a kiss, and let's Joe to the movies!

Q: What do you do when you're caught outside in a thunderstorm?

A: Hail a cab!

Q: Why was the cook fired from the sandwich shop?

A: He couldn't cut the mustard!

Q: When is a chicken a comedian?

A: When it's at the funny farm!

Q: Why was the boy firing his BB gun in the air?

A: He was shooting the breeze.

Q: Why did the fireman quit his job?

A: He got burned out.

Q: Why did the meteorologist stay in bed?

A: He was feeling under the weather!

Knock, knock.

Who's there?

Ax.

Ax who?

Can I ax you to open the door, please?

Q: What is a shark's favorite game show?

A: *Whale of Fortune.*

Q: Why did the pig get sent to the principal's office?

A: He was being a ham!

Q: Why did the vampire join the circus?

A: He wanted to be an acro-bat.

Knock, knock.

Who's there?

Toad.

Toad who?

Have I toad you lately that I love you?

Knock, knock.

Who's there?

Panther.

Panther who?

Get me a belt—my panther too loose!

Q: What happened after the boa constrictors got in a fight?

A: They hissed and made up.

- -

Knock, knock.

Who's there?

Chicken.

Chicken who?

I'm chicken under the mat for a key, but I don't see one!

Knock, knock.

Who's there?

Isaac.

Isaac who?

Isaac of these knock-knock jokes!

Q: Why did the monkey need some R & R?

A: He was going bananas!

Knock, knock.

Who's there?

Barry.

Barry who?

It's a Barry good idea for you to let me in.

Q: What is the wealthiest bird?

A: An ost-rich.

Knock, knock.

Who's there?

Hannah.

Hannah who?

Hannah over the keys so I can come in!

- -

Q: Why did the driver cover her eyes?

A: She saw the light was changing.

Knock, knock.

Who's there?

Myth.

Myth who?

I myth you when you're gone!

Knock, knock.

Who's there?

Ari.

Ari who?

Ari there yet?

Q: **Who helped the ladybug with her taxes?**

A: Her account-ant.

Knock, knock.

Who's there?

Nutella.

Nutella who?

Nutella me when we're going to get there!

Leah: Why do you have ten bowling balls?

Anna: So I'll always have one to spare.

Q: **Why did the quarterback carry a paintbrush on the field?**

A: So he could touch up his touchdowns.

- -

Q: When do you need medicine on a train?

A: When you have loco-motion sickness.

Q: What did the alien say to the soda?

A: "Take me to your liter."

Q: Why did the librarian need a ladder?

A: So she could reach the tall tales.

Q: What do you call a polar bear that makes coffee?

A: A bear-ista.

Knock, knock.

Who's there?

Juneau.

Juneau who?

Juneau I'm really looking forward to this family vacation!

Knock, knock.

Who's there?

Philip.

Philip who?

Time to Philip the car and hit the road!

Q: What's a horse's favorite snack?

A: Hay-zelnuts.

Q: **How did the flea get from one dog to the other?**

A: It itch-hiked!

Q: **Why can't a giraffe's tongue be twelve inches long?**

A: Because then it would be a foot!

Knock, knock.

Who's there?

Abel.

Abel who?

If you're Abel to open the door, I would appreciate it!

Q: How did the hog write a letter?

A: He used his pigpen.

Knock, knock.

Who's there?

Auto.

Auto who?

We auto be there by now!

Q: What did the baby orca do when it got lost?

A: It whaled for its mom!

Knock, knock.

Who's there?

Gideon.

Gideon who?

Gideon the car and let's go!

- -

Q: What is the noisiest animal to own?

A: A trum-pet!

Q: Why shouldn't horses vote?

A: They always say neigh!

Q: Why did the clown need a new red nose?

A: Because his old one smelled funny.

Q: What did the star say to the moon?

A: "I'm falling for you!"

Q: Why did the leopard visit London?

A: He wanted a spot of tea.

Q: Why did the baker keep baking?

A: He was on a roll!

Q: What do you get if your dad gets stuck in the freezer?

A: A Pop-sicle.

Knock, knock.

Who's there?

Italy.

Italy who?

Italy a long time before we stop again, so you better use the restroom!

Q: How do hogs communicate?

A: In pig Latin!

Q: What happened when the baker won the lottery?

A: He shared the dough with his friends!

Q: Why can't you trust a pig with a secret?

A: They're always squealing.

Q: What do you get when you cross an automobile and a dog?

A: A car-pet!

- -

Q: Why was the frog excited to have company?

A: He wanted to show everyone his new pad!

Knock, knock?

Who's there?

Whittle.

Whittle who?

Just a whittle longer and we'll get there!

Q: Why did the banana get fired?

A: Because he split!

Q: How did the teacher know who took the finger paints?

A: They were caught red-handed!

- -

Knock, knock.

Who's there?

Weirdo.

Weirdo who?

Weirdo we go from here?

Q: Why did Dracula need glasses?

A: He was blind as a bat.

Q: Why couldn't the astronauts park the space shuttle on the moon?

A: Because it was full.

- -

Q: **Why did Jack Frost drop out of the talent show?**

A: He got cold feet!

Q: **Why did the science teachers get married?**

A: They had great chemistry!

Q: **Why did the geometry teacher go to the psychiatrist?**

A: He had a lot of problems to solve.

Q: **When do chickens go to bed?**

A: At ten o'cluck!

Q: **When is your mother like a window?**

A: When she's being trans-parent.

Q: Why are librarians always late?

A: Because they're overbooked.

Q: Why should you keep a whale happy?

A: If he's sad, he'll start blubbering.

Q: Why did the basketball player smash the stopwatch?

A: His coach said he had to beat the clock to win.

Q: Why did the criminal duck?

A: The judge said he was going to throw the book at him!

Knock, knock.

Who's there?

Howie.

Howie who?

Howie going to get all this stuff in the trunk?

Q: Why was the girl jump-roping down the hall?

A: She was skipping class.

Q: Why did the boy put on boxing gloves before he did his homework?

A: His mom had told him to hit the books.

Q: When does a gorilla put on a suit?

A: When it's got monkey business!

Q: What is a hippo's favorite vegetable?

A: Zoo-cchini.

Q: What vegetable do they serve in prison?

A: Cell-ery.

Q: Why did the deer get a job?

A: It wanted to make a quick buck.

Q: What happened when the witch lost control of her broom?

A: She flew off the handle.

Knock, knock.

Who's there?

Wanda.

Wanda who?

Wanda go to a movie?

Q: Why did the otter do extra homework every night?

A: He was an eager beaver!

Q: Why did the grape jelly and strawberry jelly get together?

A: So they could have a jam session.

- -

Q: Why did the man go to the grocery store after work?

A: His wife told him to bring home the bacon.

Q: Why did the trombone player borrow his friend's trumpet?

A: His teacher said it's rude to toot your own horn!

Q: Why was the weatherman so upset?

A: Somebody stole his thunder.

Q: Why did the cowboy buy a new pair of boots?

A: It was a spur-of-the-moment decision.

Tick - **TAC** - Toe

CAN YOU SAIL
to the
GOLDEN GATE BRIDGE?

Knock, knock.

Who's there?

Gnome.

Gnome who?

There's no place like gnome.

Q: Why will a squirrel always keep a secret?

A: It's a tough nut to crack!

Q: Why were the pigs on the highway?

A: They were road hogs!

Q: Why did the farmer take a hammer to the barn at night?

A: His wife said he should hit the hay!

- -

Q: Why did the vampire join the army?

A: He wanted to go into com-bat.

Q: Why do potatoes make good spies?

A: Their eyes are always peeled!

Q: Why did the boy call the fire department?

A: His money was burning a hole in his pocket!

Knock, knock.

Who's there?

Jell-O.

Jell-O who?

Jell-O, is anybody home?

Knock, knock.

Who's there?

Diesel.

Diesel who?

Diesel be the best trip ever!

Q: Why didn't the corn take a plane?

A: Its ears would pop!

Q: What do you do if your walls are cold?

A: Put on another coat of paint!

- -

Knock, knock.

Who's there?

Audi.

Audi who?

You Audi let me in, it's cold out here!

Q: When is a man like a snake?

A: When he has a frog in his throat.

Q: How do you introduce yourself to a tree?

A: You shake like a leaf.

Tim: I forgot where I put my boomerang.

Scott: Don't worry, it'll come back to you!

Knock, knock.

Who's there?

Weaver.

Weaver who?

Weaver door unlocked next time!

Knock, knock.

Who's there?

Poor me.

Poor me who?

Poor me a cup of water. I'm thirsty!

Q: Why didn't King Arthur go to work?

A: He took the knight off.

Q: What does a queen wear in a thunderstorm?

A: A reign-coat!

- -

Q: Why did the captain quit her job?

A: Because her ship came in.

Q: Where do taxi drivers live?

A: In cab-ins.

Q: Why don't snakes know how much they weigh?

A: They're always losing their scales.

Knock, knock.

Who's there?

Guinevere.

Guinevere who?

Guinevere off the road, I get lost!

Knock, knock.

Who's there?

Roach.

Roach who?

I roach you a postcard from my vacation.